Hello, Family Members,

Learning to read is one of the most important accomplishments of early childhood. **Hello Reader!** books are designed to help children become skilled readers who like to read. Beginning readers learn to read by remembering frequently used words like "the," "is," and "and"; by using phonics skills to decode new words; and by interpreting picture and text clues. These books provide both the stories children enjoy and the structure they need to read fluently and independently. Here are suggestions for helping your child *before*, *during*, and *after* reading:

Before

- Look at the cover and pictures and have your child predict what the story is about.
- Read the story to your child.
- Encourage your child to chime in with familiar words and phrases.
- Echo read with your child by reading a line first and having your child read it after you do.

During

- Have your child think about a word he or she does not recognize right away. Provide hints such as "Let's see if we know the sounds" and "Have we read other words like this one?"
- Encourage your child to use phonics skills to sound out new words.
- Provide the word for your child when more assistance is needed so that he or she does not struggle and the experience of reading with you is a positive one.
- Encourage your child to have fun by reading with a lot of expression . . . like an actor!

After

- Have your child keep lists of interesting and favorite words.
- Encourage your child to read the books over and over again. Have him or her read to brothers, sisters, grandparents, and even teddy bears. Repeated readings develop confidence in young readers.
- Talk about the stories. Ask and answer questions. Share ideas about the funniest and most interesting characters and events in the stories.

I do hope that you and your child enjoy this book.

> —Francie Alexander
> Reading Specialist,
> Scholastic's Learning Ventures

For Lulu, who draws the purr as well as the fur. Thanks!
—J.K.F.

For all the little bear cubs asleep in their dens
on Pumpkin Hill at Christmas time
—L.M.

Text copyright © 1999 by Justine Korman Fontes.
Illustrations copyright © 1999 by Lucinda McQueen.
All rights reserved. Published by Scholastic Inc.
SCHOLASTIC, HELLO READER, CARTWHEEL BOOKS
and associated logos are trademarks
and/or registered trademarks of Scholastic Inc.

Library of Congress Cataloging-in-Publication Data

Korman, Justine.
    The Christmas cub / by Justine Korman Fontes.
illustrated by L. McQueen.
        p.   cm. — (Hello reader! Level 2)
    "Cartwheel Books."
    Summary: A curious cub named Pip meets an evergreen tree that explains Christmas to him, and by celebrating the holiday together they create a new tradition.
    ISBN 0-439-09833-5
    [1. Christmas — Fiction.   2. Bears — Fiction.   3. Trees — Fiction.
4. Christmas trees — Fiction.]   I. McQueen, Lucinda, ill.   II. Title.   III. Series.
PZ7.K83692Ch   1999
[E]—dc21   99-26009
                                                                                CIP
12 11 10 9 8 7 6 5 4 3 2 1   9/9 0/0 01 02 03 04

Printed in the U.S.A.   24
First printing, November 1999

The Christmas Cub

by Justine Korman Fontes
Illustrated by Lucinda McQueen

Hello Reader! — Level 2

SCHOLASTIC INC.

Cartwheel B·O·O·K·S ®

New York   Toronto   London   Auckland   Sydney
Mexico City   New Delhi   Hong Kong

A long time ago there was a cub named Pip.
He was curious about everything!

Pip lived in a big cave with his mother
and father.

One chilly day, Momma said,
"It is time to go to sleep, dear.
Winter is nearly here."

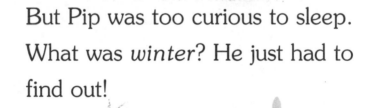

But Pip was too curious to sleep.
What was *winter*? He just had to
find out!

So he crept out of the cave and
into the wintry woods.
Pip followed his nose until he came
to a cabin.

"What is this?" the little bear
wondered out loud.
A nearby pine tree replied,
"That is a *cabin*."

Pip was curious.

"Who are you?" he asked.

"I am Evergreen," the pine tree said.

She pointed with a branch toward the

cabin. "And they are *people*."

Pip had never seen people before.

They were very interesting!

They had no fur.

And they walked on two legs
instead of four.

Evergreen knew all about people,
just as she knew all about winter.
"I'm the only tree that stays awake,"
she explained.

"I get to see all of winter.
The ice! The snow! And best of
all...Christmas!"
"What is *Christmas*?" Pip asked.

"Christmas is beautiful!"
Evergreen sighed. "The people
decorate their cabin."
Pip peeked through the window.
"I'm glad I stayed awake for
Christmas!" he said.
"But Christmas gets even better!"
said Evergreen.

"The people sing special songs,"
the tree went on.
Pip loved the music.
"I am so glad I didn't miss
Christmas!" he said.

"But Christmas gets even better!"
Evergreen laughed. "The people
bake cookies."
Pip liked the smell of cookies!
When the people were gone, Pip ate
some. He cried, "I love Christmas!"

"But Christmas gets *even* better!"
Evergreen said.

"The people give each other gifts. And it makes them feel Christmas happy."

Pip sighed, "I wish I could feel Christmas."
"I wish you could, too," Evergreen said.
And that gave the tree an idea!

The next day, Pip found a present
under Evergreen's branches.
"For me?" he asked.
Evergreen nodded, and the air
smelled like sweet pine.

Pip unwrapped his present.
"It's beautiful!" he cried.
The little tree felt Christmas happy.
"The birds helped me make it for you,"
she said.

Pip hugged his doll tightly.
"Now I know what Christmas is," said
the little bear.

But the next day, Pip realized
he was wrong.
I must find a gift for Evergreen!
the cub thought.
He looked outside the cave.
Rain trickled down from a dull,
gray sky.
What could the little bear give
to the tree?

Suddenly the clouds parted.
A rainbow appeared!
It was so beautiful!
Pip thought, *That would be a perfect present for Evergreen!*
So he ran off to catch the rainbow.

Pip found it shimmering in a puddle.
As he watched, the puddle turned to ice.
It started to snow!
Pip picked the frozen rainbow
out of the icy puddle.

The little bear couldn't wait to give
Evergreen his special gift.
But just as he reached his friend,
Pip fell and dropped the rainbow!
"I broke your gift!" Pip sobbed.

"But it is still beautiful," Evergreen said.
And that gave the bear an idea!
"Now you are the most colorful tree in
the world," Pip said.

Just then, Santa appeared.
"What a beautiful tree!" he said.
"I believe you are a *Christmas tree*."
From then on, all evergreens have been
Christmas trees—and cuddly teddy bears
have been Santa's favorite gift
to give!